M.P. ROBERTSON studied Graphic Design at Kingston University.
He is an internationally-acclaimed author and illustrator
of children's books. His many books for Frances Lincoln include
The Egg, The Great Dragon Rescue, The Moon in Swampland
and *Hieronymus Betts and his Unusual Pets*.

To Bob Gammack,
for the great times
at South Ash

The Dragon Snatcher copyright © Frances Lincoln Limited 2005
Text and illustrations copyright © M.P. Robertson 2005

First published in Great Britain in 2005 by Frances Lincoln Children's Books,
4 Torriano Mews, Torriano Avenue, London NW5 2RZ
www.franceslincoln.com

First paperback edition published in Great Britain in 2006.

British Library Cataloguing in Publication Data
available on request

ISBN 10: 1-84507-576-5
ISBN 13: 978-1-84507-576-7

Printed in China

9 8 7 6 5 4

The DRAGON SNATCHER

M.P. Robertson

F

FRANCES LINCOLN
CHILDREN'S BOOKS

Outside snow lay deep on the ground.
George nestled amongst his books.
It was a night to be wrapped warmly in
the pages of a story. As George was reading,
he was disturbed by a commotion from
the chicken house.

George peered out of his window.
Looking up at him was his dragon.
He had a worried look in his yellow eye.
George threw a blanket around his shoulders
and climbed out on to the dragon's neck.
He clung tightly as they were whisked
on the North Wind to a land that was
neither Here nor There.

Over lofty peaks they soared, until George saw
a dark castle that cut through the ice like a shard
of flint. The dragon landed silently and hid
beneath the drawbridge. George knew it wasn't
only the cold that made his dragon shiver.
There was something evil within.

George entered the castle alone.
He came to a courtyard where a soot-black dragon
stood guard. Keeping to the shadows,
George sneaked past.

He found a staircase that wound its way
up through the heart of the castle. At the top
of the stairs was a heavy wooden door.
George heaved it open.

He couldn't believe what he found inside –
shelves and shelves of frost-covered eggs.
Each was carefully labelled, from *The Rock Gobbler*
to *The Horny Cave Dweller*. They were dragon eggs!
There was only one empty space left to fill.
It was labelled:

The Lesser-Spotted
Red Crest
– extremely rare –

Suddenly George was startled by a noise on the stairs.
Quickly he hid behind a large egg.

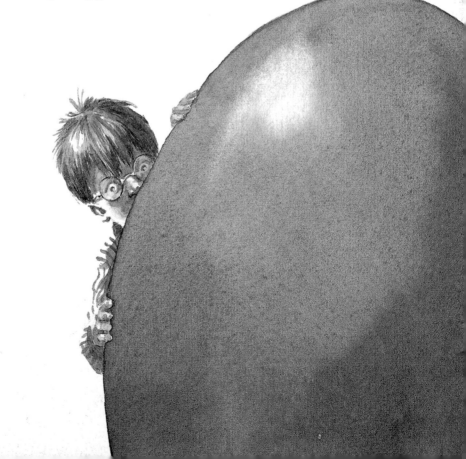

A crooked old wizard with a beard of frost entered the room. A shiver ran through George as the room became icy cold.

"Only one more to find," the wizard cackled. "Then I will rid the land of these cursed creatures."

He stared into an orb of ice, and began to mumble strange incantations. In the centre of the orb George could see the mountains surrounding the castle. The wizard searched the mountains looking into every nook and cranny. On top of the highest peak was a twisted tree. Among its branches was a dragon's nest, and in the nest was a glowing, orange egg.

"There you are, my little beauty," hissed the wizard. "Soon my egg collection will be complete!"

The wizard ran down the stairs into the courtyard
and mounted the black dragon. George leaned
out of the window and whistled for his dragon.
As it flew in front of the window, George
leapt on to his dragon's back.

They followed the black dragon at a distance.
Soon George spotted the twisted tree and – oh no!
The wizard was crawling on to a branch towards
the dragon egg.
But George had a plan. Using his blanket as a net,
he snatched the egg from the wizard's icy clutches.

Then the chase began! A ball of fire came
whistling past George's ear and crashed
into the mountainside. The black dragon
was belching fire at them.

George's dragon flitted to and fro trying
to avoid the fireballs, but he misjudged a turn
and crashed into the face of a mountain.

Luckily, George had a soft landing in the snow,
but the egg fell from the blanket and he watched
as it rolled down the mountain and landed at
the wizard's feet.

"It's mine!" said the wizard, holding the egg aloft.

But the egg began to glow as if there was
a fire inside. It burned hotter and hotter until it was
too hot for the wizard to hold. The egg was hatching!

The wizard looked on in disbelief as a tiny
red dragon emerged from the egg. Then he sank
to his knees, picking up pieces of shell.

"The last egg," he sobbed. "It's ruined!"

But the baby dragon was looking at the wizard
with love in his eyes – chirruping like a chick.

"He thinks you're his mother," said George.

"I'm not your mother, you pathetic little creature!"
said the wizard.

But as his cruel glare met the bright yellow
eye of the baby dragon, the wizard saw
the love that glowed within.
The ice that had frozen
his heart began to melt.

Back at the castle, the wizard's icy spell
had been broken. And as a new warmth filled
the egg-room, a wondrous thing happened!

The wizard led the dragon towards the castle.
     'He'll make a good mother,' thought George.
     And as he flew over the castle, a rainbow
of dragons filled the sky. George headed for home,
happy that once again dragons would fly free
in the land that is neither Here nor There.

OTHER TITLES FROM FRANCES LINCOLN CHILDREN'S BOOKS

THE GREAT DRAGON RESCUE

M.P. Robertson

When George's dragon swoops out of the sky and carries him
off to a magical land, George knows that an adventure has begun.
So when he meets a witch who has imprisoned a baby dragon,
George thinks up a clever scheme to rescue the baby
and find its dragon dad.

ISBN 1-84507-064-X

THE EGG

M.P. Robertson

When George discovers a rather large egg under his mother's
favourite chicken, he soon finds himself looking after a baby dragon.
George takes his job as a parent seriously, giving the dragon lessons
in How to Distress a Damsel and How to Duff a Knight.
But the dragon begins to pine for his own kind,
and one day he disappears…

ISBN 0-7112-1525-1

THE MOON IN SWAMPLAND

M.P. Robertson

Hidden in the dark, marshy bogs of Swampland, the wicked
and mischievous bogles hide from the Moon, and lie in wait
for travellers. Anyone who wanders too close to the edge,
will feel clammy fingers dragging them beneath the murky water.
Now the Moon has been captured by the bogles, and only
a young boy named Thomas can save her.

ISBN 1-84507-095-X

Frances Lincoln titles are available from all good bookshops.
You can also buy books and find out more about your favourite titles,
authors and illustrators at our website: www.franceslincoln.com